HALF WILD
AND
HALF CHILD

A Bertram Book

HALF WILD
AND
HALF CHILD

LIZI BOYD

Puffin Books

PUFFIN BOOKS
Published by the Penguin Group
Viking Penguin, a division of Penguin Books USA Inc.,
375 Hudson Street, New York, New York 10014, U.S.A.
Penguin Books Ltd, 27 Wrights Lane, London W8 5TZ, England
Penguin Books Australia Ltd, Ringwood, Victoria, Australia
Penguin Books Canada Ltd, 2801 John Street, Markham, Ontario, Canada L3R 1B4
Penguin Books (N.Z.) Ltd, 182–190 Wairau Road, Auckland 10, New Zealand

Penguin Books Ltd, Registered Offices: Harmondsworth, Middlesex, England

First published in the United States of America by Viking Penguin Inc., 1988
Published in Picture Puffins, 1991
1 3 5 7 9 10 8 6 4 2
Copyright © Lizi Boyd, 1988
All rights reserved

LIBRARY OF CONGRESS CATALOGING IN PUBLICATION DATA
Boyd, Lizi, 1953-
Half wild and half child / by Lizi Boyd.   p.   cm.—(Picture puffins)
Summary: Maddie and Nick, refusing to listen to their parents'
requests for them to behave, fall under a spell and become half-wild
creatures until they are able to recall how nice it was to be good.
ISBN 0-14-050825-2
[1. Behavior—Fiction.]   I. Title.
PZ7.B6924Hal 1991   [E]—dc20   90-42000

Printed in the United States of America
Set in Korinna

Away from home Maddy and Nick almost never say No.
Instead they say, "Oh yes, I'd like some more ice cream," or
"Yes, we'd like to come again. Thank you!"

But at home when Mother says, "Maddy, please brush your hair. We'll make a braid," Maddy shrieks, "No, no, no! I like wild, tangled hair!"

And when Mother says, "Nick, please brush your teeth," Nick shrieks, "No, no, no! I like dirty green teeth!"

Or if Father says, "Maddy, Nick, it's time to clean up your room," together they shout, "No, no, no! We *love* our room like this!"

One day Father says, "It's time to stop shouting and shrieking. Stay in your room. I want you to think about saying Yes rather than No!"

Maddy and Nick don't like this. They slam their door and stomp their feet. Together they sing, "No, no, no!" And with that they begin to grow purple and green spotted legs with tails! They become half wild and half child as they tear around the room.

In a while Mother calls upstairs to them, "It's too noisy up there. Maybe you'd better go out and play with your friends." Maddy and Nick like this idea. "Yes, yes, yes!" they shout. They come downstairs and are all child again when they kiss Mother good-bye.

With their friends Maddy and Nick almost always say Yes.
"Oh yes, let's play hide-and-seek," or "Yes, yes, let's go up into
the tree house!"

But at dinner when Father says, "Nick, please use your napkin," he shouts, "No, no, no! It's a milk mustache!" And when Father says, "Maddy, please take your elbows off the table," she shouts, "No, no, no! My elbows like it there!"

Mother and Father are very worried. They don't like shouting and shrieking. They would like to eat a peaceful meal. They love their children but they don't want them to be half wild.

Then Father says, "Please finish your soup and we'll take our baths," but together they shout, "No, no, no! *You* eat the soup! We won't take our bath!" So Father says, "Then you will eat cold soup for breakfast. Tonight you will put yourselves to bed. There will be no story. We cannot hear another No! Good night."

But Maddy and Nick don't seem to care. They shout and shriek as they go upstairs. They slam their door and stomp their feet.

Singing, "No, no, no! We'll never go to bed," they grow purple and green spotted legs with tails! And when Mother and Father fall asleep they go downstairs.

All night long Maddy and Nick are half wild and half child.
They tip the furniture upside down.

They spill the soup. They climb on everything. They tear the house apart.

In the morning Mother and Father wake up to find that Maddy and Nick are still awake.

Father says, "It's time to be children again." Maddy cries, "Please help us. Our wild halves won't go away. Maybe you can pull them off!" But no matter how much they tug and pull, Maddy and Nick are stuck.

Mother and Father call the doctor for the child part. They call the vet for the wild part. First the doctor pokes the wild half. Then he rubs the child half. He says to the parents, "Keep them in bed. Feed them weak tea and dry toast." The doctor is worried.

Then the vet comes in. He is very excited. He says to Mother and Father, "When they become all wild, which they are certain to do, they can come and live with us at the Animal Hotel!"

Mother and Father don't like this idea. They do what the doctor orders. Mother puts Maddy and Nick to bed. She brings them weak tea and dry toast. It doesn't taste very good.

In the darkened room Maddy climbs on a chair and looks in the mirror. "Nick," she says, "I think our wild halves will go away soon." But Nick looks up and cries, "Maddy, now we're more wild than child!"

Then Maddy lies on her bed and imagines herself living at
the Animal Hotel. "Nick," she asks, "maybe it would be fun to
live with lots of animals and roam the hotel day and night?"

But Nick grumbles, "Maddy, we don't bark and purr. I don't want to eat bones! I don't want to sleep on the floor. I want to go outside and play with my friends!" And Nick begins to cry.

Maddy climbs into his bed and puts her arm around him.
"I know, Nick," she says. "Let's think of all the things that
make us say Yes! Maybe we can become all child again."

Nick begins, "I like tree houses and my trucks and dirt too!
I like leapfrog and playing with my friends."

Maddy says, "I like my rabbit and my bears. I like birthday
parties and ice cream! I like hide-and-seek if it's not too dark,
and I like my brother too."

Nick says, "I like my sister and Mother and Father too!
I like to be tucked in and to have a night story."

Together Maddy and Nick think of all the things that make
them say Yes, until finally they fall fast asleep.

The next morning Nick feels his toes. He pulls back the blankets and jumps out of bed and shouts, "Maddy, I'm all child!" And Maddy is all child too!

Maddy gets dressed and brushes her wild, tangled hair and puts in a ribbon. Nick brushes his dirty green teeth.

Together they go downstairs and say, "We're no longer wild! We're all child!" Mother and Father are happy. Father makes their favorite apple pancakes. Nick wipes his milk mustache without being asked. Maddy's elbows never touch the table. Mother and Father raise their juice glasses in a toast: "Here's to our children! Oh, how we love you!"